Adapted by Lisa Marsoli

Illustrated by the Disney Storybook Artists

A GOLDEN BOOK • NEW YORK

randomhouse.com/kids
ISBN 978-0-7364-3019-7
Printed in the United States of America
10 9 8 7 6 5 4 3 2 1

Dusty the **crop duster** was at work in the skies above Propwash Junction. He was supposed to be concentrating on spraying vitamins on the fields, but instead he was daydreaming about racing against the fastest jets in the world.

It was Dusty's dream to enter the upcoming **Wings Around The Globe Rally**. He believed if he practiced hard enough, his dream just might come true.

After work each day, Dusty met up with
his best friend, Chug the fuel truck. He was
Dusty's **flying coach**—and Dusty needed as much
practice time as he could get.

"Okay, now let's try some tree-line moguls!" Chug said one afternoon. The qualifying race was only a few days away! Dusty expertly dipped down and rose up over a line of trees.

"That's how you do it!" cheered Chug—until Dusty started leaking oil.

Dusty went to Dottie, the local mechanic, for help. "Dusty, **you're not built to race**," Dottie said. She warned him that if he didn't stop flying so fast, he would break down—and crash!

Later, while Chug and Dusty watched a show about plane crashes, Chug suggested that Dusty get coaching help from Skipper. He was a **legendary flight instructor** who had flown missions with the Jolly Wrenches squadron in the navy.

Skipper didn't fly anymore. Instead, Sparky the tug pushed him everywhere. But Dusty agreed that Skipper might have some good advice.

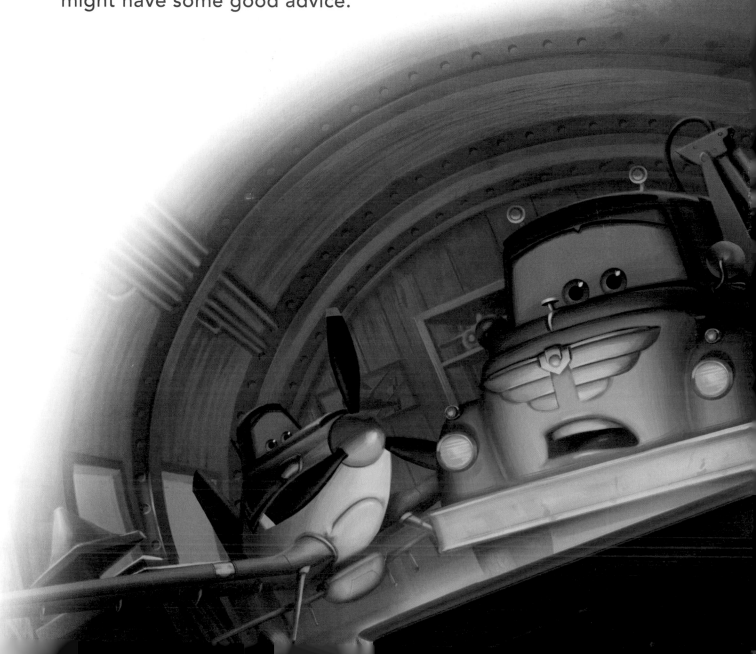

Dusty was nervous on the way to Skipper's hangar. Everyone knew the grumpy old warplane didn't like to be disturbed.

"I was wondering if you would train me," Dusty said to Skipper.

"Go home," Skipper growled. Then he slammed the door.

Dusty went to the **qualifying race** for the Wings Around The Globe Rally. To earn a spot in the rally, he would have to finish this race in the **top five**.

Dusty watched in awe as three-time rally champion Ripslinger made a showy entrance with his teammates, Ned and Zed. It was obvious that Ripslinger loved the attention of the crowd.

The race began. Dusty watched the first plane fly
through the obstacle course of pylons.
"That guy's good!" he said.

When it was Dusty's turn to try, Ripslinger made fun of him.
"You've got to be kidding me," he said. "That farmer's
going to race?"

Soon the spectators were **laughing at Dusty**, too. He tried
hard to ignore them. This was his one chance to qualify for the
rally. He had to stay focused!

Dusty roared off the starting line and **barreled toward the pylons.** He flew much lower than any of the other planes, but he was fast!

"What a finish!" announced a race official as Dusty crossed the finish line.

The judges quickly tallied the results. Dusty had **come in sixth**—not good enough to be in the rally.

Back at home, Dusty put his dream of racing aside for a few sad days. Then a rally official arrived to tell him that the fifth-place racer had been disqualified for cheating. Dusty would be **competing** in the Wings Around The Globe Rally after all!

Skipper finally agreed to coach Dusty. The first thing he told Dusty was that he would have to fly above the clouds, where the tailwinds could give him extra speed.

"I'm afraid of heights," Dusty told him.

So Skipper let Dusty fly low and race the shadow of a passenger plane that flew over Propwash Junction every day.

Soon Dusty was flying to New York, where
the **first leg of the race** would begin. All his
idols were there—twenty-one of the **fastest
racing planes in the world!** But they soon
made it clear to Dusty that the rally was not a
friendly competition.

Bulldog, an English racing champion, told
Dusty gruffly, "Every plane for himself."

Then a plane **wearing a mask** and a cape roared in.
"He's the indoor racing champion of all Mexico!"
Dusty exclaimed, recognizing El Chupacabra.
"And *número uno* recording artist, *telenovela* star,
and romance novelist," El Chu added.
Unlike Bulldog, El Chu was friendly. "We will have
many adventures," he promised Dusty.

Soon enough, it was time for the race to begin. When the flag dropped, the competitors shot into the sky and headed across the North Atlantic, where they came across a freezing storm of snow and hail. The other racers flew above the bad weather, but Dusty's fear of heights kept him close to the sea. He was shivering with cold and dodging icebergs. The crop duster landed in Iceland hours after everyone else.

Skipper told him over the radio, "You've got to try to fly higher."

That night, the racers flew to Germany.
Bulldog ran into trouble when he began to
leak oil. "Mayday! Mayday! Mayday!" he
radioed. "I'm blinded!"

Dusty rushed to Bulldog's side and **guided** him through the rest of the flight—and even helped him make an emergency landing.

Everyone admired Dusty for his good deed, but he was still in last place.

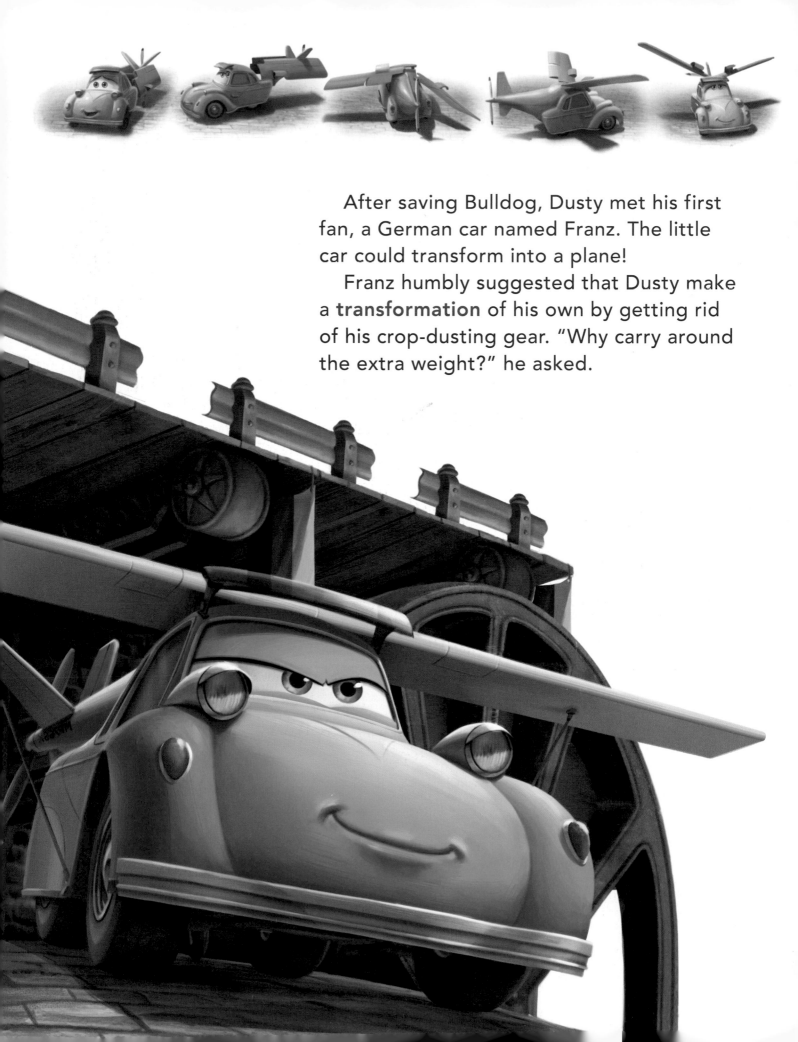

After saving Bulldog, Dusty met his first fan, a German car named Franz. The little car could transform into a plane!

Franz humbly suggested that Dusty make a **transformation** of his own by getting rid of his crop-dusting gear. "Why carry around the extra weight?" he asked.

"You need to start **thinking like a racer**," El Chu agreed.

Dusty went off to see the mechanics. Afterward, he looked—and flew—more like a racing plane.

Dusty was **faster than ever**, and on the next leg of the rally, to India, he passed one plane after another! Racing fans around the world started cheering him on.

As the racers headed into the mountains, they were not allowed to climb above a thousand feet. Dusty flew low and easily weaved through gorges and valleys. When the leg was over, he had moved all the way from **last place to eighth!**

Ripslinger fumed as the press surrounded the racing
newcomer. "Why are they wasting their time with him?"
Rip wondered. "He's a tractor with wings!"

Meanwhile, reporters wanted to know where
Dusty had learned to race.

"From my coach, Skipper," Dusty replied. "He's the
reason I'm even here. He's an amazing instructor. And
I'm sure if he could, he'd be with us right now."
Listening to Dusty back home, Skipper was inspired
to do something he had not done in a very long time.

Skipper made sure no one was around. Then he had Sparky push him out onto the runway. The old fighter took a deep breath and started his engine. Within seconds, the determination on Skipper's face changed to defeat. He shut down his engine and let Sparky take him back to the hangar.

Before the next leg of the rally, Dusty radioed home for advice. He was going to be flying over the Himalayas, the tallest mountains in the world! "What if a guy wanted to fly **through the mountains** instead of over them?" he asked.

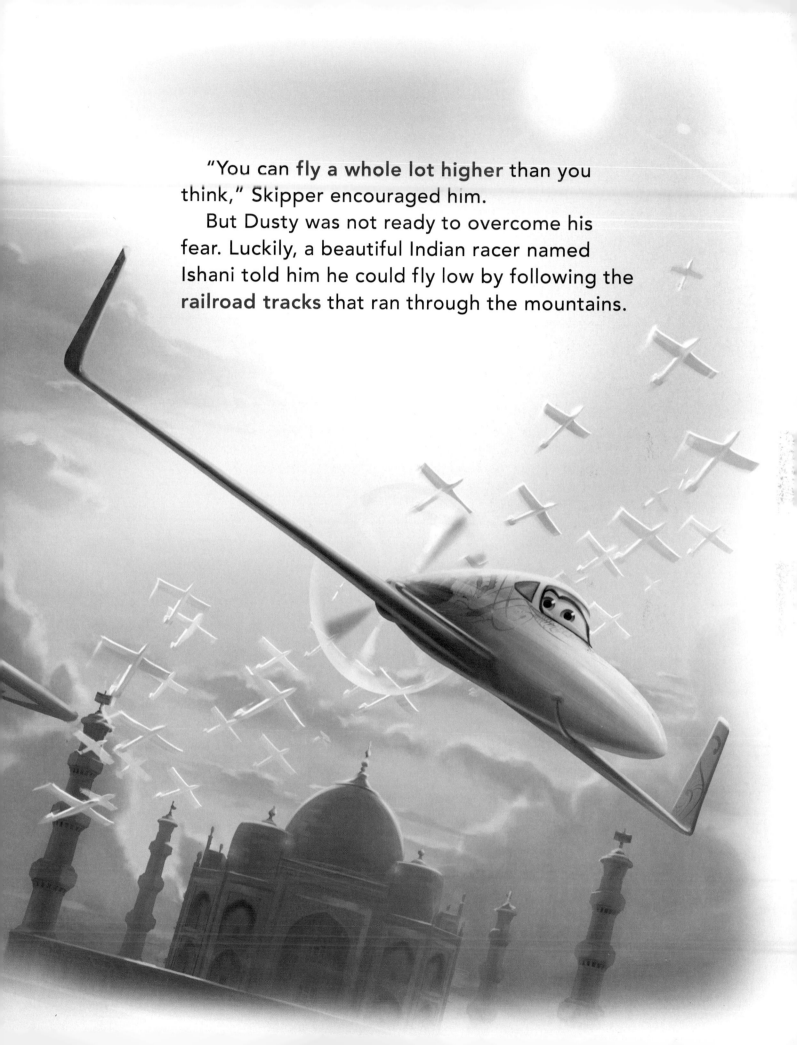

"You can **fly a whole lot higher** than you think," Skipper encouraged him.

But Dusty was not ready to overcome his fear. Luckily, a beautiful Indian racer named Ishani told him he could fly low by following the **railroad tracks** that ran through the mountains.

The next day, the racers took off for Nepal. Dusty followed the railroad tracks through the Himalayas, but he quickly discovered that they **led into a tunnel**.

Too afraid to fly above the mountains, Dusty flew inside
the tunnel—and soon heard a **train approaching**.
Dusty shot forward with every bit of power he had.

Dusty made it out of the tunnel only seconds before the train entered. He was grateful to find himself flying above the peaceful countryside of Nepal.

Soon he landed at an airfield by a monastery.

"Welcome," said an official. **"You're in first place!"**

First place! Dusty couldn't believe it.
When Ishani arrived, Dusty noticed that she had
a new propeller that was just like Ripslinger's. Dusty
was disappointed when he realized his friend had
betrayed him!

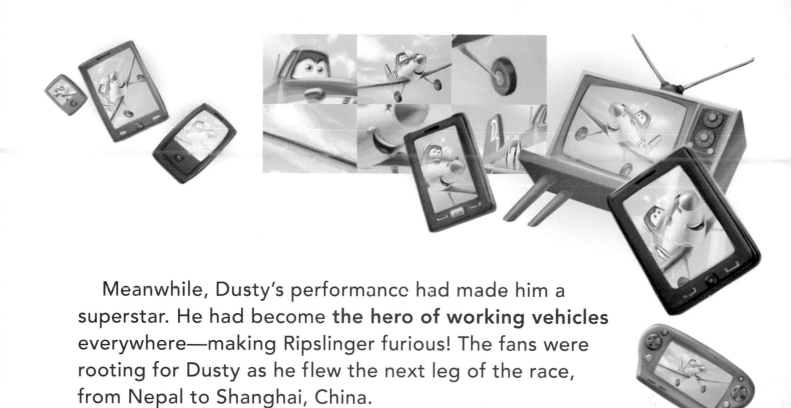

Meanwhile, Dusty's performance had made him a superstar. He had become **the hero of working vehicles** everywhere—making Ripslinger furious! The fans were rooting for Dusty as he flew the next leg of the race, from Nepal to Shanghai, China.

After arriving in Shanghai, Dusty called Skipper and his friends back home. Next, he would be flying across the Pacific Ocean to Mexico.

Skipper warned Dusty that it was monsoon season. "Be careful," he said. "And one more thing. **I'm proud of you.**"

That made Dusty feel great!

In the morning, the racers took off and quickly left Dusty behind in the fog. Suddenly, Zed swooped down and broke off Dusty's antenna, stranding him over the ocean.

Now Dusty had nothing to guide him. He spent hours
flying aimlessly—and using up all his fuel.

Luckily, two navy fighter jets, Echo and Bravo, appeared
and guided him back to their aircraft carrier, the *Dwight D.
Flysenhower*. That was **Skipper's old ship!**

On board, Dusty saw a photo of Skipper on the Jolly Wrenches Wall of Fame. His coach had only one mission listed to his name.

Dusty was confused. The way Skipper talked, it seemed as though he had flown lots of missions.

Dusty radioed home and asked Skipper about what he'd seen.
"It's true," Skipper admitted, but there was no time to explain.
A storm was brewing, and Dusty had to leave right away if he
wanted to stay in the race.

Dusty was almost to Mexico when he **crashed into the sea.** "Mayday!" he called over the radio.

A Mexican navy helicopter scooped him out of the churning water just in time.

Dusty's friends were there when the helicopter delivered him to the airport in Mexico. Despite his injuries, all Dusty cared about was knowing why Skipper had lied to him.

Skipper explained that he had **lost his entire squadron** in a battle on his first and only mission. He hadn't flown again since then.

Dusty was heartbroken—and too busted up to finish the rally.

Then El Chu appeared.

"Dusty, I cannot bear the thought of competing without you," he said, giving his friend a pair of wings.

The other racers felt the same way. They also gave Dusty parts to replace his broken ones. Ishani even gave him her new propeller.

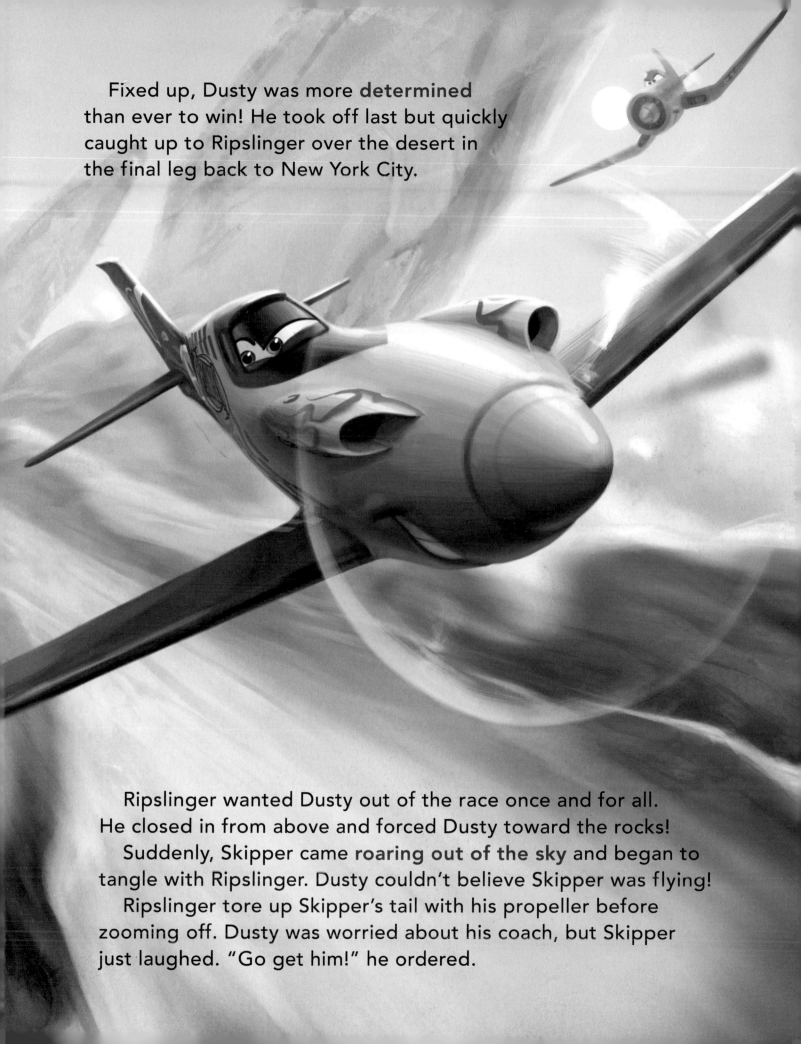

Fixed up, Dusty was more **determined** than ever to win! He took off last but quickly caught up to Ripslinger over the desert in the final leg back to New York City.

Ripslinger wanted Dusty out of the race once and for all. He closed in from above and forced Dusty toward the rocks! Suddenly, Skipper came **roaring out of the sky** and began to tangle with Ripslinger. Dusty couldn't believe Skipper was flying! Ripslinger tore up Skipper's tail with his propeller before zooming off. Dusty was worried about his coach, but Skipper just laughed. "Go get him!" he ordered.

Dusty caught up with Ripslinger, but he couldn't push past his rival. Then he gathered his courage, pulled up—and for the first time ever, **broke through the clouds!**

"Whooo!" Dusty exclaimed as the tailwinds rocketed him forward.

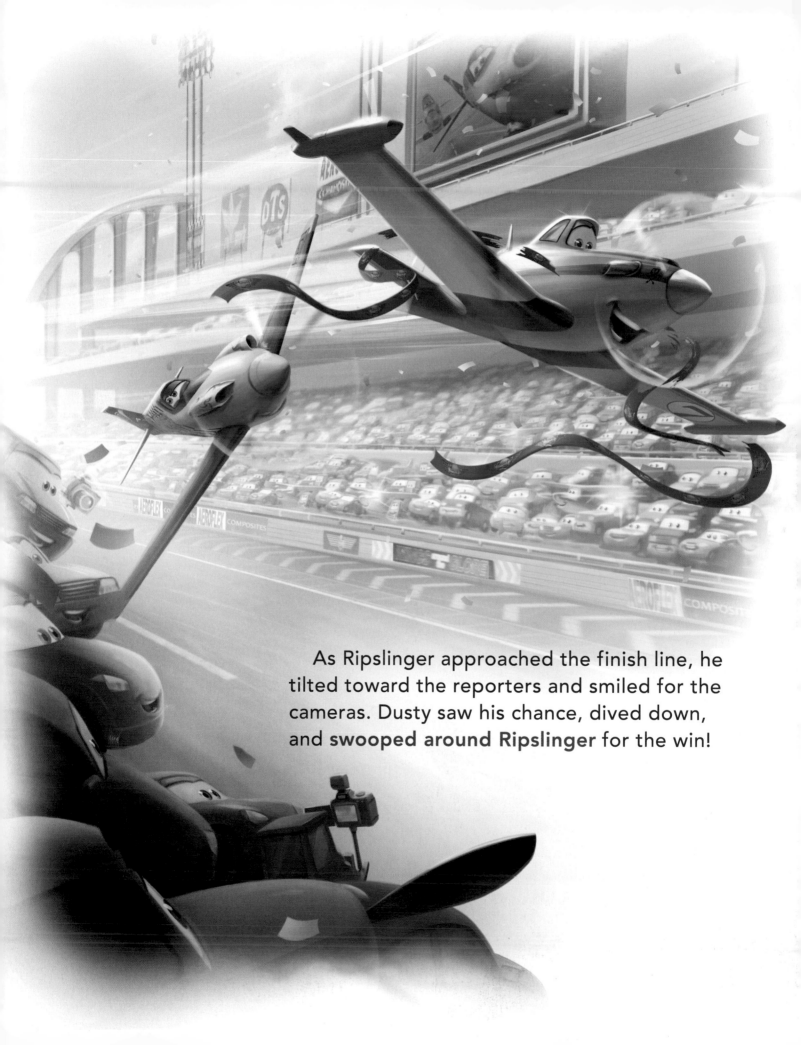

As Ripslinger approached the finish line, he tilted toward the reporters and smiled for the cameras. Dusty saw his chance, dived down, and **swooped around Ripslinger** for the win!

Dusty landed to a cheering crowd. His friends were
so proud! Dusty was grateful to all of them—especially
Skipper—for helping him make his **dream come true!**
He was truly a champion racer, and now the whole world
knew it!